For Francesca, Lucian, Benedict, and Derry
—T.M.

To my best friend, Russ
—M.S.

Text copyright © 2002 by Tony Mitton
Illustrations copyright © 2002 by Mandy Sutcliffe

First U.S. Edition

Library of Congress Cataloging-in-Publication Data

Mitton, Tony.
    Goodnight me, goodnight you / Tony Mitton ; illustrated by Mandy Sutcliffe.– 1st ed.
    p. cm.
    Summary: When it is time for bed, a brother and sister say goodnight to things both
inside and outside their house.
    ISBN 0-316-73880-8
    [1. Bedtime–Fiction. 2. Brothers and sisters–Fiction. 3. Stories in rhyme.] I. Sutcliffe,
Mandy, ill. II. Title.

PZ8.3.M685 Go 2003
[E]–dc21   2002036850

10 9 8 7 6 5 4 3 2 1

First published in Great Britain in 2003 by Orchard Books

SC

Printed in Hong Kong

The illustrations for this book were done in oil paints on paper.
The text was set in Celestia Antiqua,
and the display type is Dorchester Script MT.

Goodnight Me, Goodnight You

by Tony Mitton   Illustrated by Mandy Sutcliffe

LITTLE, BROWN AND COMPANY

New York ∽ An AOL Time Warner Company

Goodnight moon and glimmering stars.
Goodnight swish of passing cars.

Goodnight airplane in the sky,
red light, green light, winking high.

Goodnight twinkling lights so pretty
in the distant, glittering city.

Goodnight cows and goodnight sheep
drowsing quietly as we sleep.

Goodnight rabbits tucked away
in cozy burrows till the day.

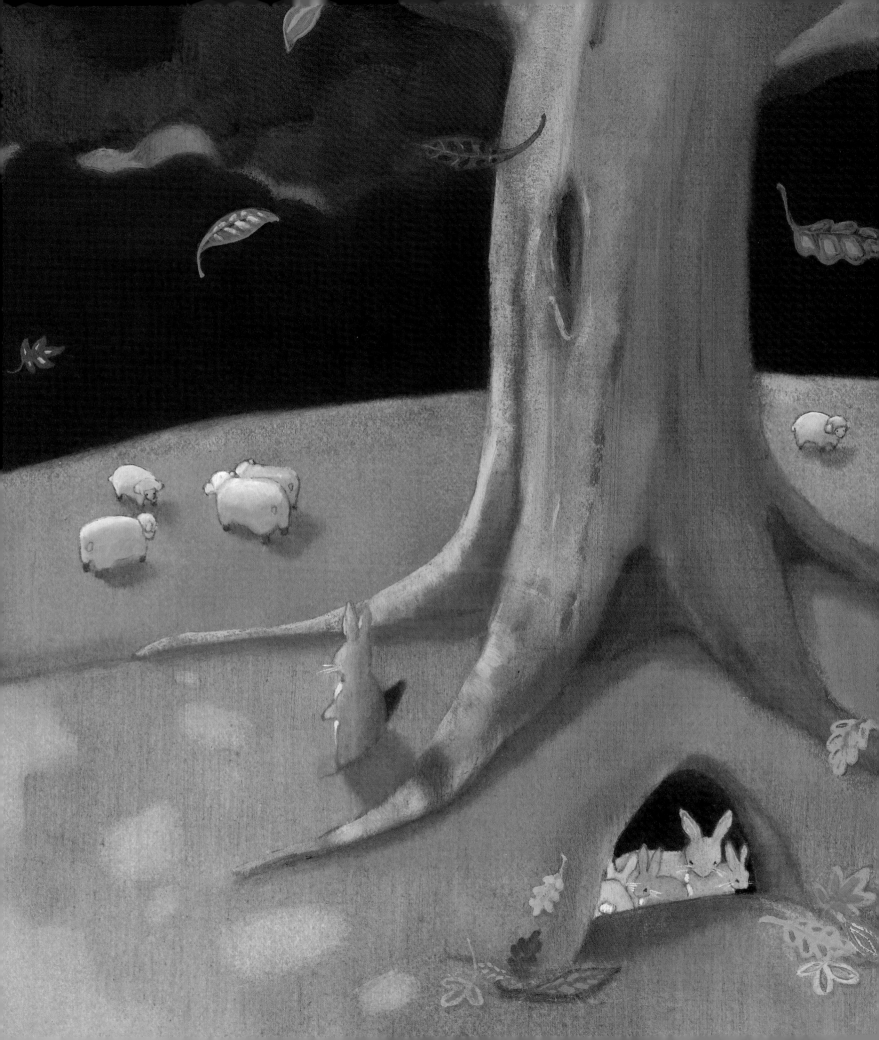

Goodnight bright-eyed birds who rest,

wrapped up warmly in their nest.

Goodnight darkness, chill night air,
beyond our window, everywhere.

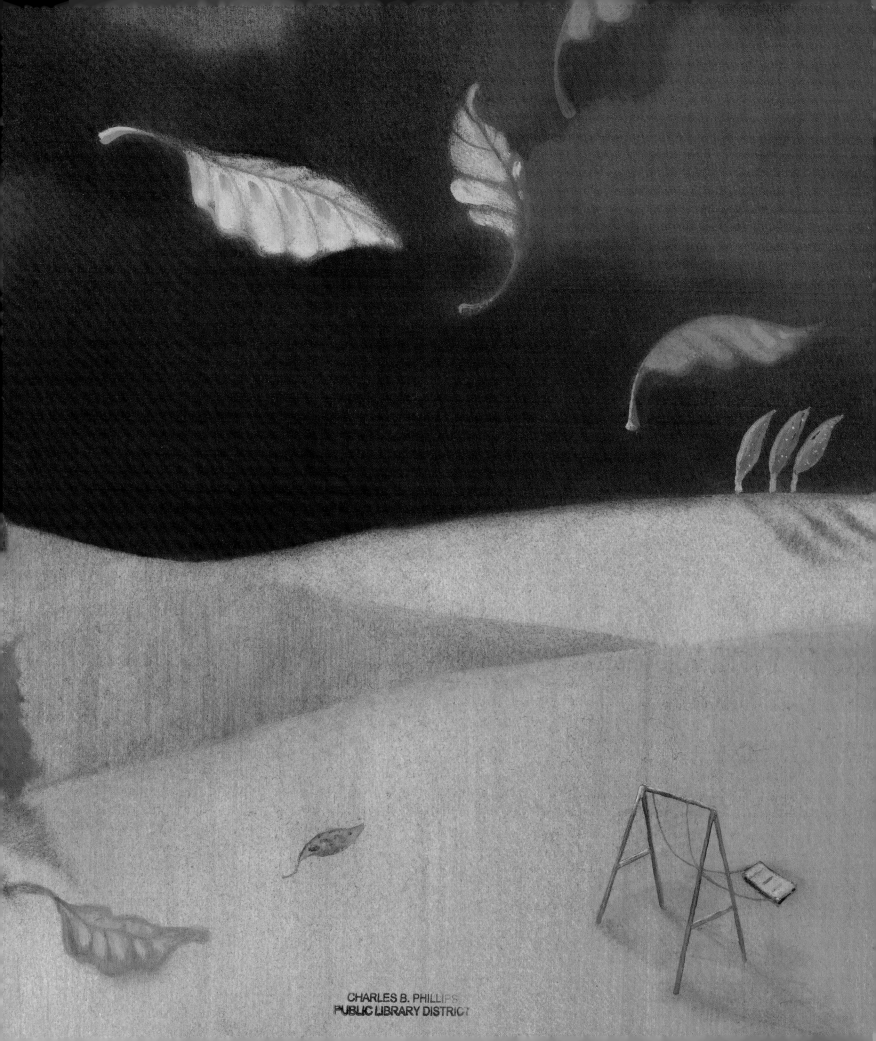

Goodnight soldiers, tall and still,

who stand like sentries on our sill.

Goodnight den of rugs and chairs,
the place we play at wolves and bears.

Goodnight pirates in their ship,
ready for the next day's trip.

Goodnight picture that we drew:
treasure island, sea of blue.

Goodnight farmyard on the floor.
The tractor rests beside the door.

Goodnight story that we've read.
Goodnight bear beside your head.

Goodnight pillow, soft and deep,
full of peace and dreams and sleep.

Goodnight kiss . . . one cheek, then two.

Goodnight me... and goodnight you.